BEATRIZ VIDAL

FEDERICO *and the* MAGI'S GIFT

A LATIN AMERICAN CHRISTMAS STORY

ALFRED A. KNOPF
NEW YORK

I wish to express my thankfulness to my dear friend Barbara Ensrud for the editing of this story.

THIS IS A BORZOI BOOK PUBLISHED BY ALFRED A. KNOPF

 Published in the United States of America by Alfred A. Knopf, an imprint of Random House Children's Books, a division of Random House, Inc., New York, and simultaneously in Canada by Random House of Canada Limited, Toronto. Distributed by Random House, Inc., New York.

KNOPF, BORZOI BOOKS, and the colophon are registered trademarks of Random House, Inc.

www.randomhouse.com/kids

Library of Congress Cataloging-in-Publication Data
Vidal, Beatriz.
Federico and the Magi's gift : a Latin American Christmas story / by Beatriz Vidal. — 1st ed.
p. cm.
SUMMARY: Because he has misbehaved, four-year-old Federico is afraid the three kings will not bring the toy horse he asked them for and, unable to sleep, he goes outside to await their arrival.
ISBN 0-375-82518-5 (trade) — ISBN 0-375-92518-X (lib. bdg.)
[1. Epiphany—Fiction. 2. Magi—Fiction. 3. Behavior—Fiction. 4. Latin America—Fiction.] I. Title.
PZ7.V6665Fe 2004
[E]—dc22
2003025880

MANUFACTURED IN CHINA
September 2004
10 9 8 7 6 5 4 3 2 1
First Edition

Para Pablo, Mariana, Federico,

Marie Eva, Nina y Leo

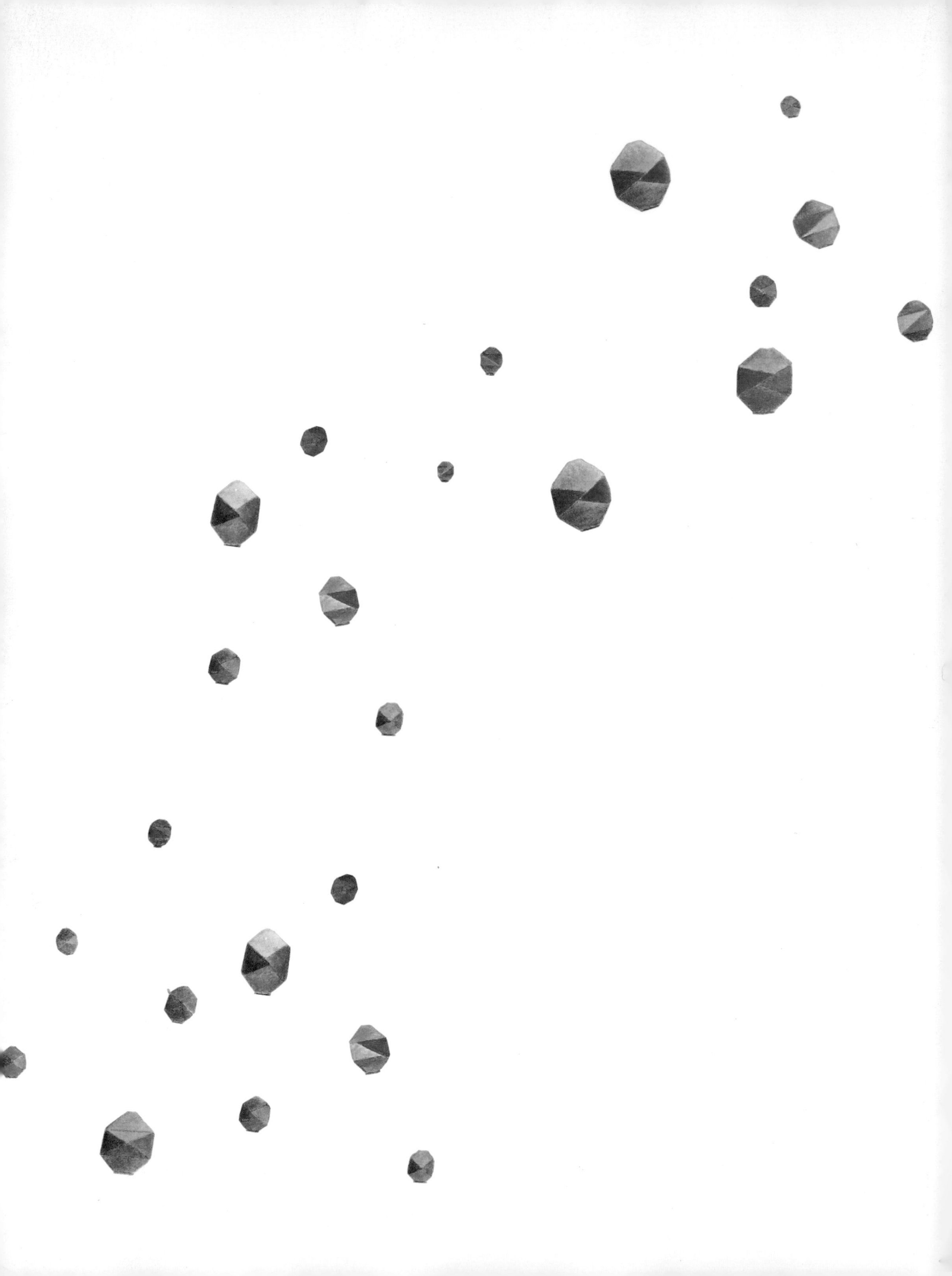

It was the fifth of January and the scent of roses and jasmine hung in the balmy air. In the small mountain village, children and grown-ups were lofting *globos* into the pale sky. Shouts of delight and squeals of laughter rang out as the balloons floated up and the sound of firecrackers greeted the end of the Christmas season.

Despite the festive feeling in the air, Federico sat motionless on the front steps of his house, staring glumly at all the activity. "With such a lovely evening," his mother said to him, "why do you have to sit here alone, in everybody's way?" Federico was four and always kept to himself when he had something on his mind.

Pablo and Mariana danced about in the yard as they looked up at the sky. Something extraordinary was going to happen that night: the coming of the Magi. Grandmother often told the story of the Magi, *los Tres Reyes Magos,* the Three Wise Men who came from the Orient bringing gifts to the baby Jesus on the twelfth night after his birth. "Ever since," said Grandmother, "the Magi ride through the night sky bringing *regalos* to good boys and girls." Every year the children peered up at the heavens with the hope of finding the Wise Men among the stars.

Pablo and Mariana began to gather hay and water for the Wise Men's camels. "They get very tired," Grandmother had told them, "and need to be refreshed after such a long journey." Federico, however, lingered on the porch. He had been scolded for misbehaving and now he was afraid that instead of the toy horse he wanted so much, the Magi would leave him nothing, his shoes would be empty.

Suddenly a voice called him. It was his father. Slowly Federico got up and went to the garden.

"Federico," asked his father, "have you written to the Magi with your wish?"

Federico nodded silently. He couldn't write yet, but he had drawn a picture of a little toy horse and his sister had written his wish underneath it.

"Perhaps if you promise the Wise Men to behave better this year, you might get your *caballito,* your little horse. Come, I'll help you." They went inside together.

When the sky was a deep blue and the stars were beginning to shine brightly, it was time to go to bed. "Don't forget your shoes," Mother said, "or the Magi won't leave any *regalos.*" Carefully, the children placed their *zapatos* out on the windowsill and then hurried to bed.

queridos
reyes
magos

Hours passed and everyone in the house was asleep, except Federico. He lay awake in his bed, nervous and worried, his mind clouded with questions:

Will the Magi get my letter in time?
Will they understand that in my heart I truly meant to keep my promise?
Will my shoes be *vacíos* in the morning?

If only I could see the Wise Men. I must try, he said to himself. He crept out of bed very quietly so he wouldn't wake Pablo and Mariana.

He tiptoed silently past his sleeping parents and carefully opened the door to the garden.

The night air was warm and fragrant with the scent of roses and jasmine.

Federico felt the soft grass under his feet. He saw the Christmas tree, the beautiful tree that Mother trimmed with silver and gold and *velas,* real candles.

He listened to every sound. He listened to the humming of crickets, to the rustle of night birds in the trees. Suddenly a dark shadow moved. He shivered. It was only Micifus, the cat, leaping at *luciérnagas,* his paws swatting at the fireflies.

Federico walked to the garden's grassy hill, where the sky stretched huge above him, a deep blue dotted with millions of stars scattered in magical forms for as far as he could see.

Birds, animals, gods, and heroes were so close that night he could almost touch them. He didn't move. He barely breathed.

And then, flickering through the stars, shining sparks of colors glittered. "Oh!" said Federico, and his heart leaped as he saw them. "It's the Wise Men," he gasped. He could hardly believe it as he counted—*"Uno, dos, tres . . ."*

And there they were: Melchior, Gaspar, and Balthasar, flying on their camels through the starry night. Angels flew alongside them. As they drew closer, Federico saw toys, lots of toys, that the Wise Men carried on their camels. "I see my *caballito*!" he cried.

Federico knew he had to hurry back to bed, for the Magi only visit houses where everyone is sound asleep. His heart was pounding as he stole back into the house.

He was so excited he wanted to wake Mariana and Pablo, but they were deep in sleep and dreams. Suddenly Federico felt sleepy. He crept into bed, and as he closed his eyes, a breeze fluttered the curtain at the window.

In the small village, everybody was now asleep as the bright stars dimmed and the night moved toward the new day.

Author's Note

In most of Latin America, the Christmas season comes at the hottest time of the year. December is the start of the summer vacation, allowing plenty of leisure for the festivities that begin with Christmas Eve and end with the Feast of the Three Kings, or Epiphany Day, on January 6. Although it has become customary to exchange gifts on December 24, Latin American children also enjoy receiving gifts on Epiphany Day.

It is the mysterious Three Magi, or the Three Wise Men, who still hold the main fascination for the children, for they are the ones who deliver the gifts on Epiphany Day. The Wise Men are invariably described as an Arab, a Spaniard, and an Ethiopian.✷ According to the biblical legend, they came from the East and followed a star that led them to Bethlehem, where they honored the new child who would become known as the Messiah, Jesus Christ.

✷Melchior of Arabia, Gaspar of Tharsis, and Balthasar of Saba, respectively

Glossary

el caballito	little horse
los globos	balloons
las luciérnagas	fireflies
los regalos	gifts
los Tres Reyes Magos	the Three Wise Men or Three Kings
uno, dos, tres	one, two, three
vacíos	empty
las velas	candles
los zapatos	shoes